My HAIR IS a GARDEN

Words and pictures by
Cozbi A. Cabrera

Albert Whitman & Company
Chicago, Illinois

To Jana, who is learning to love and appreciate
all things beautiful, including her hair.

Library of Congress Cataloging-in-Publication Data

Names: Cabrera, Cozbi A., author, illustrator.
Title: My hair is a garden / written and illustrated by Cozbi A. Cabrera.
Description: Chicago, Illinois: Albert Whitman & Company, [2018]. |
Summary: After being teased yet again about her unruly hair, MacKenzie
consults her neighbor, Miss Tillie, who compares hair care with tending
her beautiful garden and teaches MacKenzie some techniques.
Includes tips for shampooing, conditioning, and protecting black hair,
and recipes for hair products.
Identifiers: LCCN 2017041027 | ISBN 9780807509234 (hardback)
Subjects: | CYAC: Hair—Care and hygiene—Fiction. | African Americans—Fiction. |
Gardens—Fiction. | BISAC: JUVENILE FICTION / Health & Daily Living / Daily Activities. |
JUVENILE FICTION / Social Issues / Self-Esteem & Self-Reliance. |
JUVENILE FICTION / People & Places / United States / African American.
Classification: LCC PZ7.1.C13 My 2018 | DDC [E]—dc23
LC record available at https://lccn.loc.gov/2017041027

Printed in China
10 9 8 7 6 5 4 3 2 1 LP 22 21 20 19 18 17

Design by Jordan Kost

For more information about Albert Whitman & Company,
visit our website at www.albertwhitman.com.

I was always drawn to Miss Tillie's house. She lived four
houses down and across the street from our house.

There was something special about Miss Tillie. The way
she found a use for everything and made up songs while
scrubbing her porch. The way her house shone in the daylight
with its vines curling around it. It took my breath away.

You could say her house had a glory.

I used to run right into her house
when I was a toddler.

So when I was teased because of my hair—
again—it was no surprise that I found myself
running right to Miss Tillie's after school.

She led me to her kitchen table where she'd been straining sorrel. Its pungent aroma and the smell of steeping ginger filled the kitchen. When my tears came— a slow leak, a salty streak—she handed me a tissue and let me be for a few minutes.

Miss Tillie knew if I was looking for comfort, I could go to Mama for that. She knew I was at her house for a reason. She set a cup of the sorrel in front of me, and I took a sip. It went down smooth and tangy and broke through the lump in my throat.

"I...I need help with my hair," I said.

It wasn't the first time my hair had been made a joke.

I sort of got used to it. I'd shrug it off. Or I'd keep my hat on, even when I wasn't supposed to wear it in class.

But when Julio Richards, who I'd known since kindergarten, said, "We all know Mack's hair is always a mess," he said it like it was a fact. Like we all know the Statue of Liberty is surrounded by water. Or we all know George Washington was the first president of the United States.

"Folks have been poking fun of my hair since I was little,"
I told Miss Tillie. "Mama's tried to fix it, but the truth is, she
doesn't know what to do with it."

I could feel Miss Tillie's hand on my thick nest of a head. That
touch gave me hope.

I made a little song in my head.

Miss Tillie's hair is shiny.

Miss Tillie's hair is long.

She wears it as a crown

Like beauty wrapped in song.

You know, Miss Tillie's hair has a glory!

Miss Tillie called my mama, who said I could stay there a while.

Then Miss Tillie turned to me. "Now I'll show you how to shampoo," she said.

"*Shampoo?* I know my hair's a mess, but it's not dirty!" I thought.

Miss Tillie put a towel around my neck and led me to the sink.

"Normally I would part your hair in quarters before shampooing, but it's a bit tangled and matted now, so it's best to shampoo first. We'll detangle when it's more pliable. For that you'll need a wide-tooth comb."

"I already use a wide-tooth comb," I said. "Well...when I use a comb, that is."

Miss Tillie took out a large comb with teeth that looked as far apart as the spaces in a garden rake.

I nodded. "Oh right," I said, "a *wide*-tooth comb!"

"We'll use this one for now," said Miss Tillie. "Later on when your hair's trained, you can go back to your usual comb."

"Trained?" Did Miss Tillie mean she could train hair?

"Oh yes," Miss Tillie replied. "You've got to work with what you have, but you can still tell it what to do."

"Do you think my hair will be as long as yours once it's trained?" I asked her.

"Length doesn't matter, MacKenzie. Don't let anybody fool you. It's the health of your hair that counts." Miss Tillie ran the water in the sink.

"I guess you're right," I said. But I wasn't convinced. Would my hair always be somebody's idea of a joke? Would it ever be beautiful?

Miss Tillie turned the water off. "Which would you prefer if you had to choose? A healthy, shiny head of cropped hair, or hair that's long, straggly, fragile, and full of split ends?"

Were those my only choices? These questions were drowning out the song in my head.

Miss Tillie looked at me as if she were reading my thoughts. She slowly pulled the towel from my shoulder and laid it on the kitchen counter by the sink, near the drained pot of sorrel.

"Come with me," she said. She steered me toward the screen door to her garden.

Miss Tillie's backyard was a paradise with so many shades of green, bright pockets of colorful flowers and cool shade. I could barely take it in. It was as if someone had taken a big paintbrush and made bold strokes of green, then used countless little paintbrushes to fill in the details.

We walked over to a bench and sat down. I inhaled deeply. The backyard didn't smell like the rest of the neighborhood. It smelled—well, *alive*.

I wanted to know every part of this garden. I reached down to feel the ground. The earth was damp and cool. It felt like it was giving me something I couldn't see.

"How did you create this, Miss Tillie?" I wanted to know.

"Thirty or more years ago, I put some seeds in the ground," Miss Tillie said. "I planted cuttings from neighbors' and friends' trees. Bought a few plants and bulbs from catalogs."

I pointed to the tree Miss Tillie called a Japanese maple, the big one that draped gracefully over the garden. "That tree was a cutting?" I asked.

"Oh that was a wee thing at first. The phone company men came through the yard one day and trampled over it with their boots. Got in the way where they were sitting to have lunch. I found it plucked up clean and woven into the chain-link fence."

I gasped. "What did you do?"

"Oh I cried," Miss Tillie replied. "Paid fifteen dollars for that tree and that was a lot of money for me at the time. But I put that tree right back in the ground and watered it every day without fail."

I thought about how that little tree had survived and all the water Miss Tillie gave it every day, even though it just looked like a broken branch. I wondered if I would have given up and thrown it away.

I leaned down and ran my hand over some tiny plants on the ground near the bench. "What are these?"

"Those are succulents. They hold a lot of water. Makes a great ground cover."

"They sure are pretty," I said.

Miss Tillie looked at me. "Is that Japanese maple prettier than those succulents?" she asked.

"Of course not!" I said.

"Even though that Japanese maple's taller?" she asked.

"They're both beautiful," I said. "Even though they're so different."

As the words came out of my mouth, I knew that I believed it.

"Ah!" she said. "Go back inside and put your towel back on."

That was the day I first learned that my hair is a garden.

My hair is a garden. And like every good garden, it must be cared for, every day.

The nutrients in the soil can be stimulated and enriched. My body is the soil for my hair.

What I give to the soil comes back to me. I love to eat right.

My words are like seeds that I plant. What I think and speak draws a yield.

I weed out all opinions that have no place in my garden.

IT'S TOO CURLY   PULL IT BACK
STRAIGHTEN IT
CUT IT OFF

Miss Tillie says it's not what you start with in the garden that matters. It's the care, time, and attention you give it. My hair is a garden, and I give it love.

Caring for Black Hair

Shampooing

Part hair into quarters and pin or clip each section. Drench each section thoroughly with water. Apply a small amount of moisturizing shampoo to the palm of your hand and work it into your scalp gently using the balls of your fingers—never your nails. If your hair is long, hold it up while you're working in the shampoo to minimize tangling. Then pin the shampooed section back in place and move on to the next section.

Shampoo dry, curly hair no more than once a week, followed by conditioner. However, if it's summertime or you've been swimming, you may need to shampoo more often. It's best to rinse quartered hair thoroughly, shampoo once and use conditioner, or else skip shampoo altogether and go right to conditioning drenched hair.

If your hair is very dry and breaking, apply conditioner to dry hair before shampooing. Shampoo once and follow up with conditioner. With regular washing, there's no need to shampoo, rinse, repeat. Simply shampoo once.

Conditioning

Your conditioner is your secret weapon against hair breakage. Use a conditioner with high slip, which allows the hair to glide through handling.

One great trick is to use a heating cap for deeper conditioning. Or, with an adult's help, tie a recycled plastic bag over your hair and let your body's natural warmth heat your conditioner. Remove and rinse.

Sealing in Moisture

Hair needs water for moisture. You must quickly seal in that moisture. Oils, butters, and leave-in conditioners make great sealants. Finding just the right one or combination for your hair is part of the fun. What works for your best friend may not work for you.

A great sealant combats dryness, flyaways, breakage, and helps maintain tangle-free hair. If your hair is on the coarser end of the spectrum (sometimes called 4c), you may need to apply a sealant with a little more body, such as a butter, after final rinse.

Detangling

The best way to detangle your hair is to avoid tangles in the first place. That's why it's important to be careful while shampooing. Never towel blot hair—instead, place the towel around your shoulders for dripping wet hair.

Apply a leave-in conditioner or sealant to hair and gently work through to ends. Then, starting with your ends, work through smaller sections of hair using a wide-tooth comb. Handle with care, as wet, curly hair is fragile. Work through slowly, inching up toward scalp. Never tug! Spritz with water if hair dries out while detangling. Separate detangled sections by twisting gently and securing with a bobby pin or hair clip.

Once hair is styled, it's best to leave it alone until it's thoroughly dry or "set." Unraveling wet or damp hair to restyle risks more tangling and breakage.

Protective Styling

"Protective styles" are hairstyles that don't expose all of your hair to the elements or require heavy maintenance, so hair is less likely to dry out or need re-combing and less likely to break. There are many kinds of protective styles—such as braids, twists, cornrows, Bantu knots, pin-ups—and countless variations!

Trimming

Split ends are like the weeds in your garden. It's best to trim them every six to eight weeks. Trying to preserve length by ignoring split ends just causes the ends to split in other places. You may trim less often if hair length is your goal, but only if you properly care for your hair and have found a regimen that works for you.

Growing Black Hair

Most hair grows an average of half an inch each month. If your hair isn't getting longer, it's usually because of hair breakage. The most common reason for breakage in Black hair is dryness, which happens because the natural oils present in the scalp don't reach the ends of really curly hair. To prevent dryness in between shampoos, spray a spritz of water—plain water in a spray bottle will do—and apply a light oil or butter.

A daily scalp massage is a wonderful stimulant to encourage hair growth. Just make sure to use the balls of your fingers and never your nails.

There's no substitute for good nutrition: lots of water, fresh fruit and veggies, including dark, leafy greens, lean proteins, and whole grains and legumes. Make sure to get enough sleep and exercise.

Protective styles are great for growing Black hair. Wrap hair in a silk scarf or bonnet for sleeping to avoid drying out hair overnight. If you sleep with a cotton or flannel sheet, you can use a silk pillowcase. Keep hair and scalp clean, hair conditioned, and moisturized. Remember, everything responds to care!

Recipes

Herbal Infusion Rinse

An herbal infusion makes an excellent rinse that promotes a healthy scalp.

Ingredients:
10 cups cold water
1 cup dried nettle
½ cup dried rosemary
1 cup dried burdock root
1 cup dried sage leaves

Items needed:
Big pot with lid (16 cup capacity)
Measuring cup
Large stirring spoon (stainless steel or wood)
Strainer
Quart-size containers with airtight lids (3)
Spray bottle

Place water in the pot and bring to a rolling boil with the lid on. Remove the lid with a pot holder and drop in herbs, stirring to saturate. Turn the burner off, but keep the pot on the heated burner. Steep overnight. Strain into an empty pot and store the infused mixture in quart-size containers and spray bottle. Refrigerate for up to two weeks.

Great as a final rinse after shampoo. Can be used in between shampoos as a way to refresh scalp and rejuvenate hair prior to applying leave-in conditioners or sealants.

Moisturizing Shea Butter

Ingredients:
1 cup pure African shea butter
1 cup extra virgin olive oil
1 tablespoon Jamaican black castor oil
  (you may also use jojoba oil, argan oil, or avocado oil)

Items needed:
Table knife
Glass bowl (4 cup capacity)
Electric hand mixer
Measuring cup
Tablespoon

Use a hand mixer to beat African shea butter for two minutes until whipped. Scrape the sides of the bowl with a table knife occasionally.

Add ¼ cup of the olive oil and mix for five minutes. Use a table knife or rubber spatula to scrape the sides of the glass container to collect any unmixed shea butter residue.

Pour in the remaining olive oil and mix for seven to ten minutes, scraping sides occasionally.

Add Jamaican black castor oil (or substitute) and mix for thirty seconds or until fully blended. Mixture should be light and fluffy.